PALM LEAF UMBRELLA TO POORI MASALA

RANDOM WRITINGS OF V.S.KURIAN

V. S. KURIAN

ISBN 979-888521061-4

Contents

About The Author

V.S.Kurian was born and bought up in the city of Thrissur, the Cultural Capital of Kerala. The city hosts the famous Thrissur Pooram festival, which is one of the world's most colorful and spectacular religious festivals. He is now settled in Coimbatore. He recreates vivid memories of his childhood and adulthood in his writings. V.S.Kurian had been working as a Government employee. As part of his job and otherwise he has travelled a lot. Even today he loves to travel and explore lands and people. He is a voracious reader and finds interest in various fields – electronics, chemistry, music, medicine, literature, photography, and so on and so forth.

Having gained a rich worldly experience, he brings in streams of his experience into his writings. He takes the ordinary, everyday aspects from his life and highlights them. His writings are simple and interesting to read, as well as deep in thought sometimes.

CHAPTER ONE

OLAKKUDA

(An umbrella made out of palm leaf)

It was an English period in Class 11. Our English master was teaching the poem "Lead kindly light" written by the poet Cardinal Newman.

At this juncture, an unknown man, seemingly aged 40, abruptly entered into our class room. He placed an old fashioned umbrella made out of palm leaf (Olakkuda in Malayalam) near the master's table. The man soon introduced himself as the father of the student of my class Francis, who was sitting next to me. Our teacher politely asked him to call his son, and go to the verandah, if he had anything to talk to his son. But he insisted that what he had to tell must be heard by all the students of his class.

He began to speak loudly thus" In the morning, when my son started to school, it was raining slightly. So I gave him an umbrella. He refused to use that umbrella, as its cloth was slightly torn and had a hole in it. It might rain heavily in the evening. So I thought let him use this umbrella, which is not at all torn, because it is an Olakkuda." Saying this he placed the Olakkuda in the class and left instantly from the class.

It was a great moment of shame and humiliation for Francis. The thought of holding an Olakkuda itself, made him feel highly embarrassed. It was a voluminous unreasonableness inculcated upon an immaculate teenager, ready to explode at any unhappy irregularity of an orthodox society or his father. His mental attitude turned to a very severe servitude.

He began to seriously think whether he should go to his house after the class gets disbursed in the evening. If he went to his house, he should take the Olakkuda with him. Else his father would beat him with the cane kept behind the photo of St.Sebastian on the wall.

After prolonged thinking, he decided not to go home or to his angry father. He decided to go to Madras or Coimbatore. For this he had to travel by bus or train. But he had no money. At that time, he remembered his friend Thomas Kunnath's offer of Rs. 15/- for his Parker pen presented to him by his brother-in-law when he passed to SSLC (tenth standard). After looking at the Parker pen, once for all, Francis parted with the pen, and received the meager amount of Rs.15/-, which originally costs Rs.90.

Francis very soon reached Thrissur railway station. There was a train in Platform Number One ready to leave. He ran and boarded the train. As he was a travelling in the train, for the first time, he was not aware of the formalities. He did not purchase a ticket. He thought that, like in a bus, tickets will be issued in the train itself.

Till he reached Palakkad, no Ticket examiner came to check the tickets. At Palakkad an examiner came and checked. Francis had no tickets. The examiner also coveted the small amount of Rs.15/- that Francis had in his pocket, and asked him to get down at the next junction, which was Coimbatore.

Accordingly, Francis got down. An old man, who had no ticket, was also asked to get down. So Francis and the old man both got down in Combatore at about 9 p.m. They both slept in the railway platform. Before sleeping Francis narrated his distressing story to the old man.

Next morning, the old man advised Francis to search for a job in hotels, so that at least he would freely get food three times a day. Just opposite to the railway station, there was a hotel. Both of them entered inside. They had two idlis and one tea each. The old man paid the bill.

The old man asked the hotel manager, whether Francis could be employed there. The manager told that they require one boy to clean the table and wash the vessels. Thus Francis, who should have studied further and should have been well placed, became a table cleaner in a hotel.

Very many boys in the explosive age group of thirteen to nineteen leave homes due to lack of awareness of their fathers and aggressiveness of their sons. Actually these sons crave for much love and affection from their fathers during their teen ages. The fathers too love them at heart, but are unable to express it in the proper or desired manner. I would not term it as generation gap, but it is lack of knowledge of the psychology of growing teen age boys.

CHAPTER TWO

An Unexpected Explosion

There was a new subject called 'Everyday Science', when I was studying in 9th standard. The science behind everyday things was taught to us in that class. One day, while explaining the properties of Nitric Acid, our Master, casually told us that Nitric acid will explode with the sound of a big cracker (Elephant cracker) by just adding one drop of glycerin to it.

Here my thoughts went astray. I thought, instead of buying crackers which are costly, I could make explosive crackers with high sound, with this wonderful idea of nitroglycerine. For the preparation of this compound, I had to buy two chemicals namely Nitric acid and Glycerin. Hence I went to Velukkaran's chemical shop located in Swaraj Round South in Thrissur to purchase them.

When I returned to my home with these chemicals, there was Antony Kaavalakkadan, waiting for me. He was one year younger to me and his father was a Bank Manager. Antony was my nearest neighbor and my closest friend. He used to come to our house daily in the evening to play. When I told him about this interesting incident, he showed much eagerness to see the result.

So we both went to the backyard of our house with some minimum necessary accompaniments. There lay an old hand grinder (known as Ammikal in South India and Sil Batta in Hindi). In a metal cap of a small bottle, I took some (2 c.c.approximately) nitric acid and the same amount of glycerin. I slowly mixed them both. Then placing this metal cap with the two chemicals on the ammikal, I hit on the ammikal with an iron hammer, as suggested by our Chemistry Master. But to no purpose! No explosion took place. We were at a loss to know what to do next.

Then Antony suggested to take a little of this mixture in a small bottle and shake it. Without much thinking or hesitation I did the same and shook the bottle. Oh! With a very high sound, the contents of the bottle exploded, producing a sound equal to that of dynamite. We have heard such a loud sound only during the famous Thrissur Pooram festival fireworks. Everybody inside our house came out to the backyard. We were a joint family with eighteen members. Fortunately both of us were not injured.

But the new shirt of Antony became like a fishing net with full of small holes caused by the burning of the shirt cloth by nitric acid spray. Antony had great worry not for burning his body, but for his costly shirt, which was bought by his father recently for the annual church festival. Those days getting a new shirt was not an everyday affair. So Antony was scared to go home for fear of being beaten up by his father.

Poor Antony decided to remain in our house till dusk. He hoped that in the darkness nobody will notice the dilapidated state of his new shirt. He went home at night. His plan worked out. He escaped from the notice of his mother and others on that day. But later when his mother took the shirt for washing, she saw the tiny holes all over his shirt. When she asked about this to Antony, he disclosed the truth to his mother with a pathetic appeal not to say about this mishap to his father. His affectionate mother consented to her dear son's mellifluous request. Thus Antony escaped from a painful punishment from his father.

As William Goldmsith says "The sweetest sounds to mortals given are heard in Mother, Home and Heaven." God could not be everywhere and therefore he made mothers. A mother's love towards her child is legendary. No wonder why the famous novelist Thackeray, the author of 'Vanity Fair' says "Mother is the name for God in the lips and hearts of little children".

CHAPTER THREE

From Chennai to Coimbatore with Shame

Many years back, I was returning from Chennai to Coimbatore by Kovai express after attending an official work.

I was comfortably seated myself in the allocated seat. People were making exits and entries into the compartment with bags and suitcases. The train had to leave within the next ten to fifteen minutes. One gentleman came to me. In a low soft tone, he requested me to have an eye on his two green suitcases, placed on the luggage rack, as he had to go out to the platform. I agreed.

Then showing me a currency note of Rs. 500, he asked me, "Have you got change for Rs. 500?" I told him, "Sorry, I have hardly hundred rupees as change." Intending to give me the Rs. 500 note he said, "You keep this 500 note and instead give me that Rs.100. You can give me the change later". At this moment, a ticket examiner greeted the gentleman and asked "Where are you going Mr. Mehta?"

"To Bangalore" the gentleman said. "By this train?" the examiner asked doubtfully. "I'll get down at Jolarpet and get the Bangalore train". Saying this Mr.Mehta left out in a hurry forgetting to give me the Rs.500 note. I showed my ticket to the examiner.

Time was nearing for the train's departure. I waited for Mr.Mehta, whose two green suitcases had been entrusted to me. I had also given him 100 rupees. The train left.

After one hour, the train reached Arakonam. A family of two children was getting ready to get down. The father took the two green suitcases. I told him the matter. The father in an angry tone said, "This is my luggage. If anybody has claimed them as his, he must be a rogue. Where is he?" I told him that he got down at Chennai and did not turn up. I told him the story about my 100 rupees too. Then he said that it is that fraud's routine way of cheating people.

Meanwhile another ticket examiner came, and asked for my ticket. I showed him. He looked at me suspiciously and asked in a hollow deep tone "Why are you showing me last week's ticket?" I told him that I had purchased it that morning. Also 1 informed him that the other examiner, who had checked my ticket in Chennai did not say anything.

"The other examiner?" exclaimed he. "Who is that?"

I then knew that the first duplicate examiner had changed my ticket and had given me an old one, which I did not notice. He was a friend of Mehta. So he helped Mehta in diverting my attention. I was told by the examiner, that, Mehta will return my new ticket to the Central Railway Station counter at Chennai, before the train leaves, and receive 75% of the value of the ticket after deduction. They were treacherous villains of Central Station at Chennai.

However I suggested that these stories of cheating should be made known to the public through loud speakers on platforms for the safety of passengers.

I was ashamed to think that, I had been doubly cheated in this way. Thus I reached Coimbatore from Chennai with shame!

CHAPTER FOUR

ALL ABOUT A CAT

May I confess, that the title of this article will suggest it is an imitation of A.G. Gardiner' s very interesting and humorous essay 'All about a Dog'. When Keats planned to write an epic (HYPERION), he took Milton for a model. Deciding to spruce up my writing style, I adopted the 'Gardinersque style; its felicitous and impressive language impressed me much. So I tried to create a situation with a cat for a humorous write-up which should delight all readers; but after hours of imagining I could make no progress. Then it occurred to me that I was least competent to produce a delightful essay, Witty as well as wise, like A.G. Gardiner.

At this juncture I remembered the words of Wilson Mizner, an American wit and dramatist. When you take stuff from one writer it is plagiarism; but when you take stuff from many writers it is research". So I moved to the path of such a research. For me, there are equally humorous favourites like Stephen Leacock (With the Photographer) E.V. Lucas (Tight Corners') Among these intellectual personalities, Goldsmith ranks first in my list, His immortal presentation of Beau Tibbs, The Man in Black, Doctors etc in 'The Citizen of the world' are the most lovable and thought provoking. They take form in the "Chinese Letters" supposedly written by a Chinese Philosopher who had arrived in London in the 18th century.

Now I decided to follow his style. But the very word 'Chinese' brought before me a subject, which gave me a theme to the first quarter of my article. My 'Chinese' youth pen, a popular brand fills me with savage envy for its sheer beauty. But as every rose has it's thorn, - this youth' has a Sloth! - This self-filling pen poorly accommodates ink. As a result frequent refills arrest my flow of thought. The pen has undoubtedly caught my fancy. It tempts me to write about youth. I have heard a general statement that Youth is a blunder, Manhood a struggle, Old age all regrets. Byron said, "The days of our youth are the Days of our glory"

Youth is of course, proverbially a period of dreams. Visions, ideas and ambitions which may appear to a mature mind to be exceedingly ridiculous or absolutely impracticable, haunt our minds. In youth, we run into difficulties, in old age difficulties run into us. To Wordsworth "To be young was very heaven" (The Prelude XI). But youth rushes in where angels fear to tread! Sometimes the lives of such youth become a catalogue of lamentable blunders. However I believe, it is highly pessimistic a creed to hold that youth is a blunder. To support me The Bible inspirits us thus "Rejoice, O young man" (Ecclesiastes XI 9).

And from profound thoughts on youth, my brand of "Youth" in shambling style chooses to explore the regions of forgiveness in the life of a practical minded Sheik who forgives his son's murderer by rewarding the latter with gifts of gold and a horse with the incredible words of wisdom:

"Thou art avenged my son, sleep in peace" By loving his enemy the Sheik also sleeps everyday in peace.

And from thoughts on peace to piecemeal valves, my pen in an offensive mood disapproves of the 'catish title' that neither soars the mind nor fills with humour but slinks away in lazy fashion to platitudes of every day usage that brings difficult issues to easy ends as "Man proposes and God disposes". The rewards for so rambling an exercise as my pen has dared to write on, I beg not to visualize, Perhaps this has been the similar lurking fear of all celebrities literary or otherwise who have allowed themselves to be carried away by the first flushes of an ambitious pen and to a writer tasting of the delights from the Pyrenian spring, my essay like life, begins from somewhere and goes nowhere. We hope to become somebody but rarely reach anywhere. As the poet Long fellow put it:

"Our ingress into this world
Was naked and bare
Our progress through the world
Is trouble and care;
Our egress from the world
Will be nobody knows where".

CHAPTER FIVE

ENUKAAYA

Enukaaya is the upper most banana or plantain in a bunch. It is also the largest one in the bunch. This is to describe an incident that happened while I was in college.

Those days I was studying at a renowned college in Thrissur. Till Intermediate classes (Plus one and Plus Two) the students can study in the main campus. B.A classes are in another block. Opposite to this block is the house of the Chakolas. The B.A block building has a 5 cent plot in its backyard.

It had four coconut trees, a few banana trees and one plantain tree. The plantain bunch on the tree was almost ripe and looked tempting. When we saw it, Kunnathu Paramban Thomas, the most naughty and funny person in our group, came up with an idea. He suggested that we can cut a hand of plantains (many bunch of plantains), dig a hole in the yard, place it inside and cover it with soil. This will help the plantains to ripe faster. All of us liked the idea.

We required a machete knife to cut the plantain branch and also needed a long spade to dig the hole. Chirakkal Jose said that both of these can be organized from the home of the Chakolas. He walked straight to their house. An elderly maid was sweeping the floor of the house. Jose went and said "Ammaamma(grandma) can you please open this gate?". The maid got irritated by the way she was addressed (Grandma). In a furious tone, she asked "Who is your grandmother? I am not so old. I will only be 70 years old in this coming month of Makara. Just call me Chetuthiyare (sister) ".

Jose called her accordingly and requested her to lend a machete knife and a spade for an hour. When she asked the reason, Jose told her that it was to do a small gardening work. Jose immediately approached the villains waiting in the college yard. One of them dug a big hole in the ground. Another one cut a bunch of plantains and buried them in the pit. The day was a Sunday. The next Thursday was Gandhi Jayanthi and the college would remain closed. So we decided to gather in the same place at 5.00p.m on Gandhi Jayanthi day to eat the ripe plantains.

At that time, one of our classmates Kochuanthony asked, "Can I too come?" So Jose sarcastically said, "We need someone to pick up the peel of the plantains. You can come for that purpose. We will not give you a single plantain to eat". Hearing this Kochuanthony left the place in anger and shame.

On October 2nd, at five o'clock in the evening, we arrived at the college grounds. We removed the plantains from the pit. It was ripe and looked delicious. The sharing process started. Everyone began to argue that they wanted the 'Enukaaya" (the largest fruit in the bunch). As the argument was continuing, an unusual voice from behind said, "I need the Enukaayaa".

The voice was that of our Rev.Fr.Principal. Kochuanthony stood beside him. We all knew that he had taken revenge upon us. Principal Fr. was accompanied by car driver George. Fr. ordered. "Give those plantains to

George. Then tomorrow all six of you just come to my room in college at 10.00 a.m, meet me and then go to your classes". Everyone began shivering at the thought.

The next morning, we assembled before the Principal's room at 9.30 a.m. We looked at Thomas and asked him the means to escape. He said "Don't worry. I will take care of everything. You enter the Fr.'s room very sadly. I will enter later in even greater sorrow. Then see what happens"

The five of us entered first. As soon as Fr. saw us, he asked, "Have the Panchpandavas come? Where is Lord Krishna?" Thomas then entered. He came crying loudly and beating in his chest saying, "My fault, my fault, my most grievous fault. My fault, my fault, my most grievous fault." Fr. was at a loss as to what to do when he saw this unexpected behaviour. Fr. told us "Hold him. He is going to hurt himself badly by doing this. Take him along with you and go to your classes."

Thomas' plan worked out. As we were walking out of the room, thinking that we had escaped, Fr. called us. "Wait, I have something to tell you. You think what you had done yesterday is a joke. But you have violated the Tenth Commandment of the Bible - not to covet another's property. You have committed a crime on the day of Gandhi Jayanti. Do not be enslaved to such temptations anymore. Ask forgiveness from God, and get back to your classes. I would also like to tell you one more thing. Do not consider Kochuanthony as a spy. He is just a reason for you, to not go from small mistakes to big mistakes in life".

Those words still linger in my mind. Today, among those six, some are proficient. Everyone else lives decently. May be if it weren't for our beloved Principal, we wouldn't have reached anywhere in our lives and would have taken wrong paths and reached wrong destinations.

There are many people in our lives who play the role of secret agents of God. One of them was our loving and respectful Principal Fr. I still remember him with gratitude.

CHAPTER SIX

DADDY'S DELUSION

(written in the year 1997)

I notice, dear Daddy, the sorrows of your changing face.
   Where smiling spring and moonlight bloom once did grace.

Now you are withered to a man pale and bony,
   Without a car, bungalow or Bank Balance for money.

Who cares for you, Daddy?
   Who wants to be upright like you?

Who cares for good character and clean thoughts
   When money alone is the barometer in courts.

Who considers your Christian charity?
   Who loves your Victorian etiquette?

Erudite wisdom and elaborate knowledge
   Are of no material value to acknowledge.

Who wants it all?
    You are an unsuccessful man, Daddy

You couldn't secure a cozy status
    Hawala, urea and cattlefeed are unknown to you.

How I wish you had strong guts, Daddy
    To smuggle kilos of gold from Dubai

And you know, I'd proudly say
    "My Daddy is a Jewellery Business Magnate".

But you've always remained to be
    A sort of hardworking person like a bee

Spending unlucky hours in chemical experiments
    Cosmetic research and electronic gadgets.

Only to become an unsuccessful man.
    My friend disowned her father on this count.

But never, never will I do that.
    Never Never will I forsake thee DEAR DADDY.

It will be ingratitude of the highest order
    Which will like an undertaker, draw me to life's border,

Yes I want an upright father, like you. Daddy
    You never need anticipatory bail or VIP's Jail.

CHAPTER SEVEN

LET MY COUNTRY AWAKE

(written in the year 1998)

"Into that heaven of freedom, my Father,
 Let my country awake!"

Prayed Tagore in his 'Gitanjali' before 1947;
 After fifty years of Independence, Let me pray:

Where Woman is without fear
 and rape is quite unheard of,

Where pretty brides do not die due to
 merciless 'bursting' of dowry stoves,

Where, for sorcery, witchcrafts, and demonology
 innocent children are not put to homicide,

To that heaven of freedom, O Father,
 Let my country awake !

Where administration moves without corruption.
    without Hawala, Harshad Metha and Urea,

Where the Titan Bribe does not hurl India into Tartarus
    to lay its Octopus hand in every field,

Where the guardians of citizens do not become
    the puppets of leaders and criminals,

To that heaven of Manuneethi Cholan,
    O God Let my Country awake !.

Where exploitation by medical profession
    Ultra Sound Scanning for Whitlow of finger,

Where human kidneys are not stolen
    for insatiable thirst for filthy lucre,

Where spurious drugs do not kill by punch
    The credulous patients inch by inch,

To that Olympus of Hippocratic oath, O, God
    Let my country awake!

Where Cain does not kill Abel
    Raman does not murder Rahman

Where fanatics do not massacre the humble
    in the name of Gods of those people,

Where religious amity and human love
    make this earth a magnificent paradise,

To that paradise of Milton, O Father,
    Let my country awake!

CHAPTER EIGHT

CHEST PAIN ON ASKING TO GOD

My uncle's daughter was getting married at Thrissur in Kerala. I started by train from Coimbatore with my mother my elder sister and her two daughters to attend the marraiage.

Any train journey through Kerala is a wonderful feast for the eyes. When we pass through those valleys, beautiful landscapes move backwards and new sceneries of green palms and dancing bamboos appear before us. Those who have a poetic mind to enjoy these natural sceneries will have a sumptuous nourishing food throughout the travel. One would be reminded of Keats' saying 'A thing of beauty is a joy forever'. Nearby you can see the greenish paddy fields, yonder areca nut and coconut trees, and beyond these you can enjoy a bird's eye view of the Western Ghats providing sweet sensations of idyllic beauty.

As usual the train was very much crowded. When we entered into the compartment, there was no seat to sit. One gentleman was sitting near the window. Placing her head on the lap of that man, a woman (might be his wife) was lying on the full bench, allowing no space for anybody to sit there. She said to my mother "One person can sit here". My mother modestly sat near her legs.

Then the husband said "She is not doing well. She is suffering from chest pain. That is why she is lying down." Immediately an old man sitting in front of her bench said "This lady has no pain or illness. This man is lying. Till now, she was happily talking and laughing loudly. Just to lie comfortably on this bench, she acts as if she is suffering from chest pain". Hearing these words, I politely requested her if she could sit, so that my sister and her two daughters could sit. But she vehemently refused and continued to lie there.

We reached Palakkad. At this juncture, I saw my friend Mr.Madhavan Nair, a railway police constable walking on the platform. So I complained to him about the anomaly. Madhavan asked the lady to get up and sit. But immediately her husband said "She is suffering from severe chest pain". Believing it to be true, Madhavan Nair told to me "As she is sick, let her lie down. You kindly adjust for another hour". The lady looked at me and gave me a sly, victorious smile. Large amount of odiousness had been packed in the smile of that ostentatious woman.

The train began to move in high speed. We were passing through a forest. Suddenly the engine driver began honking horns continuously and the train came to a sudden halt. A herd of elephants were crossing the track and the driver had to apply the brakes suddenly, to avoid hitting them. But unfortunately this sudden halt, caused the fall of one big leather suitcase from the upper berth. It landed exactly on the chest of the woman lying down on her husband's lap. It inflicted severe chest pain on her. The faked chest pain became a real one.

In the meanwhile, the train reached Thrissur junction. We got down at the junction thinking about the sad plight of the woman, who was now suffering from genuine chest pain. My mother uttered a sincere prayer requesting God to save her and protect her. What an irony, I thought. But then I realized, this prayerful requisition is what God expects from each one of us – to love our enemies.

CHAPTER NINE

A Lizard in My Life

This incident happened during the time I was residing in Saibaba Colony, Coimbatore. My daughter was just admitted to First Standard. As she is my only child, I did not send her to LKG and UKG, in order to have her fond presence more at home. I had also intended to experiment, what would happen, if these innocent children were not sent to school at this very young age. I always feel sorry for these kids, who are treated like caged birds, when they ought to enjoy the love and affection of their parents. So at the age of five, she was admitted directly to First Standard in a Convent school in Coimbatore.

Now as I said earlier, this incident of the lizard happened during this time when she was just admitted to the school. One day I was getting ready to go to my office. When I came out of my residence in Saibaba Colony, a lizard fell right on my head, just from above the entrance door. My thoughts were led astray. I have heard that falling of a lizard on one's head is an obnoxious ill-omen. They say that death will be the immediate ill-effect on the part of the unlucky person, whose head was "ornamented" by the unwelcome puny creature, the lizard.

Believing that, it was my last living day, I was engulfed in sorrow. I did not mention about the incident even to my wife, for the simple reason that I did not wish to worry her too. I decided to have one last glance of my daughter and walked towards the school, where my child was studying. When I reached the gate of the school, students were going in a line after the Prayer Assembly and saw my little daughter near the entrance of the corridor. There I had a last sight of my daughter, once for all, I thought.

Bearing a mountain of grief, I left the school. Throughout the day fear gripped me. I could not concentrate in my work. The day seemed to me to be longer than usual. Finally somehow the day ended. I went to bed praying to God. The next day morning I woke up. My joy knew no bounds. I thanked and praised the Lord in gratitude.

Today I am happy, that I am able to narrate this story to my daughter's son. It became clear to my mind that no lizard or any other creature can influence our life or destiny. Only God Almighty can control our day to day affairs and bless our life with bliss and peace.

CHAPTER TEN

MEMORIES

My daughter was a working woman. It was my wife and I, who took care of my grandson when she would leave for her job. She would leave my grandson at our home when she leaves in the morning and would pick him up when she comes back after work in the evening. He was an adorable toddler. As he was our only grandson, we used to treat him as our prince. Nevertheless my grandson used to miss his mother. At one point of time, he began to miss his mother very badly.

So the minute my daughter leaves for work he would start crying, "Mamma, mamma, I want to see her". Even if we divert his attention for a while, he would again start "Mamma, mamma, I want to see her". My wife began to feel sad and worried. I could never bear the sight of him crying. I decided to do anything on earth to pacify him. With this began a new routine in our life.

We stay in a place called Edayarpalayam in Coimbatore. The minute my grandson begins to cry, I would carry him out with me, and board a mini bus from our place to Vadavalli, which is about 2kms far from our place. From Vadavalli we would board 1C bus and take a ticket to Ondipudur, which is the terminus of 1C. So thereby he will not cry during this one hour bus journey. I will show him all the vehicles and sights on the road. We will get down at Ondipudur bus stand. The minute we get down, he would again start asking for his mother. So I will buy him one tea and a snack(bajji, bonda, vada etc.) He will have it happily. After loitering around for some time, we will board the same 1C from Ondipudur to Vadavalli. Again he will not cry for the next one hour bus journey.

After getting down at Vadavalli, we will board a mini bus and reach home. The minute we reach home, he will again start in a low tone "Mamma, Mamma" and start crying. So I would carry him again for sight-seeing on the main road. One day as were walking like this, we saw a baby goat. He got so excited. He told me, that he wanted to catch it. Initially I refused. But as I said, earlier, I would do anything to avoid upsetting him. I agreed. So carefully he started to run behind the small goat. It ran faster. With my help, he caught the goat. We carried it home. My wife was astonished at the sight. . She told us that the owners are going to come in search of it. But my grandson sharply refused to let it go. The goat began to cry. My grandson plucked some leaves and gave it to eat. But the little goat refused.

After some time we could hear the cry of a big goat. It was standing outside our gate and was crying. It happened to be the mother of the baby goat.

Yet my grandson was not ready to leave the little goat. So my wife told him "Kutta (which means little boy), You feel sad, when your mother goes to work, and you get separated from her, isn't it?. The same way the little goat would also miss its mother. Be a good boy, and let out the goat"

These words struck him. In his little mind, somewhere he felt that he and the baby goat were sailing in the same boat. He immediately opened the gate, and let out the goat. The little one ran to its mother. Its joy knew no bounds.

The mother and child instincts are the same in all God's creations. Motherly affection is something divine and unsurpassable. Millions of children, born to working mothers, miss their mothers very badly and the vice versa too. Yet to make a living, these mothers take a hard decision in their lives.

CHAPTER ELEVEN

GLASS - HANDLE WITH CARE!

My native place is Thrissur. Our residence is in Palakkal Angadi (adjacent to the southern compound wall of Civil Hospital). So my parish is Basilica of Our Lady of Dolours (Puthan Pally). It is one of the biggest and tallest churches in Asia. It is famous for its Gothic style architecture. The annual parish feast of this church is on the last Sunday of November every year. It is celebrated in an extravagant pompous manner. Natives of Thrissur, especially Catholics living in various places outside Thrissur used to come to celebrate their parish festival without fail.

Things being so, I also started from Coimbatore with my elder sister, wife and my daughter aged four in the morning train – Trivandrum Mail. The train arrived in the platform. As my sister was an aged person, she could not walk fast. When she was coming slowly on the platform to get into the train, one tea vendor came running with a tray of eight glasses of tea. He came in such a hurry and dashed on my sister. She fell on the platform. Asking my wife and child to get into the train, which was ready to leave very soon, I helped my sister to get up. As we were rushing to get into the train, the tea vendor held me, asking the money for the broken glasses. I told him the mistake was his and as such I need not pay any compensation. He was not agreeable. At this juncture, one police constable on duty at the platform interfered into the matter and told me that I need not pay any money to the tea vendor.

But during this quarrel, I did not attend to the train, which was slowly leaving the platform. We could not get in. My wife and child were in the train. As there were no mobile phones those days, I ran with the train and shouted to them to get down in the next station which was Podanur.

My child was very much panic struck. Innocent little one began to cry thinking that I was lost or caught by the police. She asked her mother, if the police would beat her Daddy. All the passengers in the train began to take pity on my daughter, as nothing could pacify her and she continued to cry loudly. They tried to pull the chain and stop the train. But later left the attempt, as the train was about to reach the Podanur junction.

At Podanur junction, my wife and child got down as instructed by me. The Railway Police Inspector, who was on duty, saw my wife and child. My child still continued to cry. She thought she would never be able to meet her father and aunt again. Seeing them in such a condition, he enquired the whereabouts to my wife. On enquiry he knew that it was my wife and child. He knew me already as I was working in the same Railway Department. He phoned to Coimbatore station and asked a staff to inform me that my wife and child had alighted at Podanur station and were safe. He also informed that he would bring them in his jeep to Coimbatore station in half an hour, as he had a duty to attend in Coimbatore Railway station. All the while my child still continued to cry. Within thirty minutes, his jeep came with my wife and child.

When my child found me, she was extremely happy. She began holding my hands and started kissing me. The joy of being lost and found is amazing and incredible.

The pangs and suffering of the families of the missing members or children due to abduction or various other reasons is something inexplicable and unbearable. It is more painful than death. Let us pray for such people and wish for happy endings with reunited families living happily ever after.

The festival of my native church Trichur, could not be attended or enjoyed due to this unexpected mishap nor could we breathe our native air as poet Alexander Pope sang "Happy the man, whose wish and care....Content to breathe his native air..."

CHAPTER TWELVE

POORI MASALA

When my daughter was five and half years old, we decided to send her to school and admit her in First Standard. Till then we did not send her to Kindergarten classes, because I always felt sorry for the tots who missed their parents and family very early in life. So we took our daughter to a reputed English medium convent school for the admission interview.

The interview was in English. She was asked to recite a rhyme. She did not utter a word as she could not comprehend the language. We speak Malayalam at home. In the next round she was asked to say the numbers from 1 to 20. To this question also she stood stand still. The last and final round began. A few colours were displayed on the table. The Sisters who were conducting the interview pointed out to a particular colour. My daughter was expected to say the name of the colour in English. Though my daughter did not know a word in English, these colours excited her. So when the sister pointed out to the first colour, she said "pacha" meaning green in Malayalam and when the second colour was pointed out she said "manja" meaning yellow. The Sisters began to laugh out loudly.

We were asked to wait outside for the next round of interview with the Principal. My wife and I began to feel that it was a foolish decision to have retained our daughter at home, without sending her to school for the past two years. As we stood there regretting, we were called inside. The Principal Sr. was a stern lady but was at the same time humane. Though she chided us for our foolish decision, she accepted to admit my daughter in the reputed school. My wife and I thanked her a lot and left home.

The school reopened. Everyday my daughter would throw tantrums to go to school. She would not understand a word that is taught to her in school. When the teachers and other children communicated with her in English, she would not respond as the language was new to her. Days passed. The first term exam was conducted and in ranking, she was the last in her class.

She was also a very shy child. Whenever somebody comes home, she would go and hide under the table or behind my wife. One day my friend's family came home with their daughter. Their daughter Nisha was my daughter's classmate. When my daughter saw them, as usual she went and hid under the table. My wife asked her to come out. But she refused. Nisha was a smart kid. She spoke only in English. She was the first rank holder and my daughter the holder of last rank in their class. Nisha was the class leader and would often bully my daughter. When my friend's wife asked her to recite a poem, she immediately did it. My friend looked at me proudly and told me that I should have communicated in English at home, in order to make her smart. When the family left, my daughter gradually stepped out. My wife and I felt sorry and disappointed for my daughter.

On that day we decided to face the challenge and bring her out of her shell. In the meantime, the second term of school exams was fast approaching. My wife began to spend hours with my daughter teaching her and inspiring her. The efforts paid off. She scored third rank in class. Her class teacher was astonished and gave her a beautiful pencil as a gift. My daughter began to feel a bit confident. In the annual exam of the same year she scored first rank.

My wife and I felt very happy. Of course these ranks and grades in First standard do not decide one's future, but it helped in a great deal to boost the morale of my daughter. As a token of appreciation for her performance, we took her to Annapoorna hotel for the first time and bought her a plate of Poori with Potato Masala. She relished it and loved it. Eating at hotels was a luxury those days, especially for the middle class.

There was a speech competition in her school, when she was in second standard. The topic was "Indira Gandhi". As she had scored first rank, her class teacher selected her for the competition from her class. Being well aware of her shy nature, we were a bit worried. However we decided to accept the challenge. I prepared a speech for two pages. My wife taught her the entire speech. Within a short span, she learned it by heart. She began narrating it without leaving a word. On the day of the competition, she was quite worried to go to school. My wife kept motivating her by saying "You can my dear child. If you cannot, then who else can?"

To our surprise, she bagged the first prize in the speech competition. Our joy knew no bounds. When we reached home in the evening, we took her to Annapoorna hotel and bought her Pooris. Throughout her school life she participated in almost all the cultural competitions. I would reach home from office and sit for late hours in the night, preparing her speeches, debates, essays and so on and so forth. My wife would sit with her, motivate her and help her in all of this. On many occasions, I had to take her to distant places for inter-school competitions. Though there were hassles, I stood firm to my purpose. She would secure prizes in most of the competitions. It became a custom in our home to go to Annapoorna for a plate of Poori Masala to celebrate her achievements.

She maintained the first rank consistently in all the classes. She became the School Pupil Leader and was also the First rank holder in our District in Standard Twelve.

The Sisters of the Convent school in which she studied still continue to fondly call her as "Pacha Manja".

Today she addresses large crowds and gives them motivational speeches and talks. Before leaving for any important programmes, she still continues to discuss the content with me over phone. Whenever she expresses any apprehensions my wife continues to motivate her saying "You can my dear child. If you cannot, then who else can?"

Last week, she had sent me a photo in Whatsapp with the caption "Guess who?'. It was a photo of my daughter speaking on the stage and a lady in blue saree among the audience, jotting down notes. The lady in blue saree was Nisha.

Deep in my heart I felt a great sense of satisfaction and uttered a prayer of gratitude to God, for being with my daughter through this journey. My wife and I called our daughter immediately and asked her if we could go to Annapoorna for a plate of Poori Masala.